Down by the Station

BY WILL HILLENBRAND

SCHOLASTIC INC.

New York Toronto London Auckland Sydney
Mexico City New Delhi Hong Kong

RAIL CROSSING ROAD

W9-CCW-386

No part of this publication may be reproduced in whole or in part, or stored in a retrieval system, or transmitted in any form or by any means, electronic, mechanical, photocopying, recording, or otherwise, without written permission of the publisher. For information regarding permission, write toPermissions Department, Harcourt Brace & Company, 6277 Sea Harbor Drive, Orlando, FL 32887-6777.

ISBN 0-439-21625-7

Copyright © 1999 by Will Hillenbrand.
All rights reserved.

Published by Scholastic Inc., 555 Broadway, New York, NY 10012, by arrangement with Harcourt Brace & Company.
SCHOLASTIC and associated logos are trademarks and/or registered trademarks of Scholastic Inc.

12 11 10 9 8 7 6 5 4 3   0 1 2 3 4 5/0

Printed in the U.S.A.   08

First Scholastic printing, September 2000

The illustrations in this book were created in mixed media on vellum, painted on both sides.
The display type was set in Belwe Bold Condensed.
The text type was set in Worcester Round Bold.
Designed by Kaelin Chappell and Will Hillenbrand.

To Liz; Charlie;
my wife, Jane;
and my son, Ian

Down by the station
early in the morning.

See the little puffer-bellies
all in a row.

See the engine driver
pull his little lever. . . .

Puff, puff,
Toot, toot,
Off we go!

Down by the elephants
early in the morning.
See the little calf
waiting to go.
See the engine driver
pull his little lever. . . .

Puff, puff,
Toot, toot,
Thrump, thrump,
Off we go!

WINGS OF THE WO

Down by the flamingos
early in the morning.
See the little chick
waiting to go.
See the engine driver
pull his little lever. . . .

Puff, puff,
Toot, toot,
Thrump, thrump,
Peep, peep,
Off we go!

Down by the pandas
early in the morning.
See the little cub
waiting to go.
See the engine driver
pull his little lever. . . .

Puff, puff,
Toot, toot,
Thrump, thrump,
Peep, peep,
Grump, grump,
Mew, mew,
Flip, flop . . .

DANGER

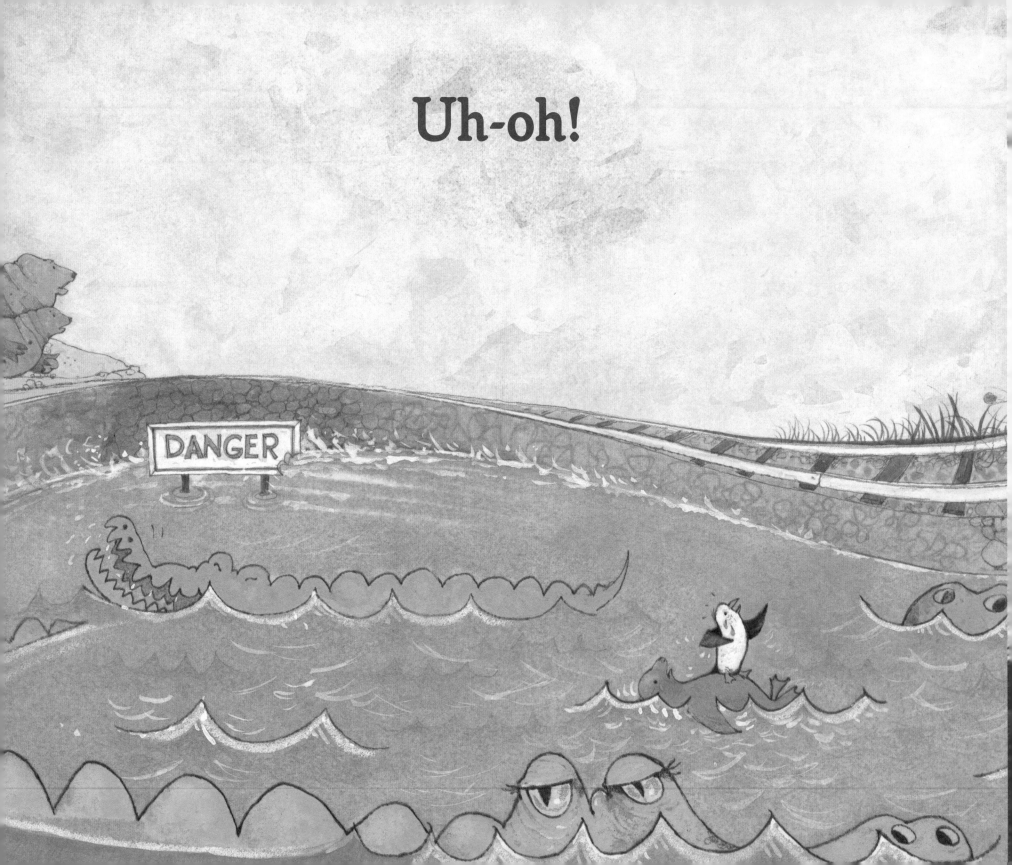

Phew!

Down by the kangaroos
early in the morning.
See the little joey
waiting to go.

See the engine driver
pull his little lever. . . .

Puff, puff,
Toot, toot,
Thrump, thrump,
Peep, peep,
Grump, grump,
Mew, mew,
Flip, flop,
Bump, bump,
Off we go!

Down by the children's zoo
early in the morning.
See the baby animals
exit in a row.
See the engine driver
pull his little lever. . . .

Puff, puff,
Toot, toot . . .

Off we go!

Down by the Station